GW00726898

cry of the
Karri

Also by Errol Broome

Dear Mr Sprouts

Tangles

Rockhopper

Nightwatch

Splashback

What a Goat!

Quicksilver

Tough Luck

Magnus maybe

Missing Mem

cry of the Karri

Errol Broome

ALLEN & UNWIN

First published in 2001

Copyright © Errol Broome 2001

All rights reserved. No part of this book may be reproduced or transmitted in any form or by any means, electronic or mechanical, including photocopying, recording or by any information storage and retrieval system, without prior permission in writing from the publisher. *The Australian Copyright Act* 1968 (the Act) allows a maximum of one chapter or 10% of this book, whichever is the greater, to be photocopied by any educational institution for its educational purposes provided that the educational institution (or body that administers it) has given a remuneration notice to Copyright Agency Limited (CAL) under the Act.

Allen & Unwin
83 Alexander Street
Crows Nest 2065
Australia
Phone: (61 2) 8425 0100
Fax: (61 2) 9906 2218
Email: frontdesk@allen-unwin.com.au
Web: http://www.allenandunwin.com

National Library of Australia
Cataloguing-in-Publication entry:

Broome, Errol.
Cry of the karri.

ISBN 1 86508 401 8.

I. Title.

A823.3

Cover photographs by David Flockhart
Cover design by oid design
Text design by Sandra Nobes
Typeset by Midland Typesetters
Printed in Australia by Australian Print Group

10 9 8 7 6 5 4 3 2 1

cry of the karri

The author wishes to acknowledge advice on bushwalking from *Paddy Pallin's Bushwalking and Camping*. (Paddy Pallin Pty Ltd, Sydney 1985)

Thanks to Department of Conservation and Land Management, Western Australia, for information on the State's forests.

In a cottage at the edge of the forest, a family of three sits down to eat. A fourth place is set at the table for someone who isn't there, someone who doesn't come.

blisters

WITH EVERY STEP, he felt himself falling. Yet his feet were still on the ground.

His body was here, on the forest path, but his mind kept dragging him into other places. Only his feet led him on, following Dutchy and Titch, not caring if he caught up with them, yet knowing he couldn't go back. Home wasn't a place Aiden wanted to be right now.

The pain of Sabina's scream still echoed in his ears. Would he ever forget her twisted mouth and the eyes black as midnight that knifed through him as she fell?

He hadn't meant to push her off the verandah. He knew as soon as she fell that he hadn't wanted to hurt her. Or had he? The scenes replayed inside his head . . .

the jab to her ribs, the scream, the panic in his chest. Calling Mum, calling the doctor, calling Steve from work, everyone calling, and speaking to him politely, saying it was an accident. No one blamed him.

The shock on her face haunted him as much as the shock inside himself that he could have done such a thing.

He skidded on the soft track, and found his stepfather close behind him.

'I'm still here,' said Steve. 'You're okay.'

He wasn't okay. If only he could wipe away yesterday. This hike would be fine if he could stop brooding over what he'd done to Sabina. And if he didn't have blisters on his heels.

For weeks, Aiden had looked forward to the long weekend in the national park. Steve said he could bring two friends, so he'd asked Dutchy and Titch to come too.

Good old Dutchy, who lolloped along, minding his own business. Not like Titch, who couldn't help minding everyone else's. Dutchy gave the feeling he'd never let you down. There was always a smile hiding on his pudding face, waiting to show he was your friend. You'd pick Dutchy every time to come on a camp like this, and somehow you'd end up with Titch as well.

That was the trouble with Titch. He knew how to worm his way into things; and it helped that his mother and Aiden's mum were friends.

Now, Aiden couldn't look his stepfather in the eye. Each time he stopped beside Steve, Aiden turned his head away. He was waiting for him to ask, Why did you do it? and he hadn't worked out an answer. He couldn't explain. It's all inside me, was all he could think to say.

'You're lagging!' called Titch.

Aiden pulled a face at him. Titch was always fifty strides ahead in his special hiking boots and the right sort of socks. Aiden knew he'd read every bushwalking book and trained like an Olympian for this weekend. He'd seen him puffing up and down stairs at school. For the past month, he'd carried a brick in his schoolbag, and walked home instead of riding his bicycle with his mates. He was a bit of a try-hard, Titch.

Stuff him! Here he goes again, thought Aiden. Titch stopped, waiting for the others to catch up. He had their routine all worked out as if he, and not Steve, were in charge. 'The book says, "walk for one hour, rest for ten minutes. Have a drink and an Anzac biscuit to keep up your energy."' Titch pulled the healthy, homemade biscuits from his backpack, and offered one to Steve and Aiden and Dutchy. Aiden took one. The crisp oats

3

turned to grit in his mouth and his stomach tightened into a knot. He chewed on and on, all the time seeing Sabina's startled face in front of him and the sickening splay of her legs as she fell.

When they stopped for lunch, Titch took off his boots and stretched his toes. He nodded to Dutchy and Aiden. 'Take 'em off, so your feet cool down. It's not a bad idea to air your socks, too.'

Aiden loosened the laces on his boots, but there was no way he'd take them off. He could feel blisters where Mum's darning had rubbed against his heels, and he didn't want to look. The sight of red, raw skin would make it even harder to start walking again. It was only Saturday, and they had two more days to go.

He gritted his teeth, half in pain and half in anger. Mum hadn't bought him hiking socks, but had mended his old football socks instead. She'd sent him off camping with socks that gave him blisters. Yet only the week before she'd bought Sabina two new pairs. He couldn't shake that from his mind.

'Take 'em off,' said Titch again.

'Shut up, Titch! Stop bossing me around!' Aiden ached to take off his boots, but it wasn't only his heels that were hurting. He wished he hadn't invited Titch. He had a way of turning good things bad.

Aiden had to stop himself from jerking out his elbow and knocking Titch off his perch. Titch caught the look in his eye, and leapt to his feet. Aiden eased himself up, and they stood face to face, but not eye to eye. Aiden stared over Titch's head to show him what a little squirt he was. Then he felt mean having done it. Titch couldn't help being small. But he could help trying to know everything.

'Just pipe down,' said Aiden and slumped back on the log.

The two boys stared at Aiden, surprised at his outburst. Steve made signs to them to keep quiet and not say any more. Aiden saw the frown on his face. He could imagine what Steve thought of him now. Shame burned deeper inside his stomach.

I mustn't limp, he told himself. Blisters were nothing. Nothing, compared to a broken leg.

He'd pushed Sabina without thinking, because of the way she looked at him. She'd tilted her nose and half closed her eyes as if she'd rather not see all of him. And she kept on brushing her hair while he talked to her; crinkled, dark, blue-black hair like her father's, though Steve's had started to go grey at the temples.

When he grew up, Aiden wanted to be like Steve. Mum's friends said Steve loved Aiden as if he were his own, and Aiden had believed it until Titch made him doubt it.

It seemed such a long time, but was only three weeks ago that Titch told him what he'd overheard. 'My Mum said isn't it lucky that Steve had a girl and you were a boy.'

'Why?' Aiden couldn't see the point.

'Because if Sabina was a boy, *you* wouldn't be so special.'

The revelation blew all the breath from his body. Of course! Sabina was Steve's, and Aiden was only the boy who came with Mum seven years ago when she married Steve.

Having a sister the same age had been fun till Titch said that. It set him thinking, and he began to notice things. Like the night Mum said, 'Clear the table, Adey,' even though it was Sabina's turn.

'Sabina has a debate tomorrow,' said Mum. 'She needs to work on it tonight.'

'I have things to do, too,' he said.

Steve jolted the back of Aiden's chair. 'Get up, Aiden! You each get your turn.'

He landed all the dirty work. Sabina was perfect in their eyes. He knew his face was pinched and grumpy that night. No wonder they liked her better.

Trust Titch to tell him! He'd never have had the sense to work it out for himself. Steve had always been kind to him, laughing with him, helping him with his maths, taking him outside to kick a football. But from that day Aiden began to see his stepfather differently.

If I didn't like him so much, I wouldn't care, he thought.

Steve had stayed at the hospital most of the night. 'The surgeon says her leg will be fine,' he told Mum and Aiden. Was it only *this* morning?

Aiden thought Steve would call off the hike. After all, Steve was Sabina's father, not his. But Steve didn't want to disappoint anyone. He'd planned the trip weeks before, and there wasn't another long weekend for months. They'd only be away three days, and Sabina was in good hands. Still, Aiden felt pretty bad going off camping when his stepsister was in hospital with her leg in a plaster cast. All because of him.

Yes, blisters were nothing. But they stung when he stood up, and he stumbled when he tried to walk without a limp.

'What's up, mate?' asked Dutchy.

'Nothing, I'm okay.'

Titch streaked out in front. Steve stayed behind, so he could watch the boys. Before they set out, he'd said they would walk only as fast as the slowest one. 'If the slowest one leads, no one gets lost.' Aiden was sure, even before the blisters, that he'd be the one in the lead, holding the others back. But Titch couldn't wait, so Steve let him go ahead.

If it hadn't been for Titch, there might never have been troubles at home. The small germ Titch had planted in his head had grown and festered until it burst apart.

'Let's keep moving,' called Steve.

Aiden nodded, without speaking. Each time they reached a fallen log or muddy stretch, he felt himself slipping further behind. They entered a track, dwarfed by karri trees taller than some city buildings. He stopped to look about him, sensing other dangers lying hidden in the forest, waiting to trip him up or drag him down. He felt as if he were walking into something; something shadowy he didn't understand. And he could do nothing to stop it.

'Look up!' said Steve.

Aiden rested against a massive trunk. The branches reeled against the sky. Clouds swam past, tilting the trunks towards him. It made him giddy to look.

'The streets of London were paved with some of these timbers,' said Steve.

Aiden ran his fingers over the blue-grey bark. Blotches of yellow and orange made the trunk look as if an artist had been at work. The forest stretched ahead, its columns melting into a crowded darkness. Titch was a tiny speck among the trees.

Steve pulled a map from his pocket to check their camping spot near the centre of the park. 'Cockatoo Corner, that's where we're heading. We'd better get a move on, to beat the rain.'

A false dusk enclosed them as they wound between the karris. Ferns and scrub covered the ground, where shriketits darted across their path. A fairy wren flitted among the leaves in a flash of blue and red.

In the depths of the forest, they heard a soft clitter-plink, as if it came from another place. But when they emerged into the open, they felt rain on their faces.

'All hands to the tent, before we're soaked!' said Steve. 'Aiden, you get the fire going. Titch and Dutchy, you're cooks tonight!'

Aiden helped hammer tent pegs into the ground, and threw the backpacks under the shelter of canvas. Water dripped off his nose and ran down his neck. He shook drops from his face and blew them with a bit of spit in Titch's direction. He grinned at Dutchy. 'Would you believe, I've got dry paper in my pack?'

There was dry wood, too, under cover beside the fireplace. Aiden waited till the rain stopped before he set the campfire. When he pushed his nose out of the tent, the air smelled as if it had been whisked with a broom. Drips slid from leaves and glistened on bracken fronds. Somewhere through the understorey, the trill of water told Aiden a creek wasn't far away.

His fire crackled to life and flames licked the logs before sinking into a glow of red coals. Steve said it was the best campfire he'd seen since his scoutmaster days. Aiden stifled a sigh of relief that he'd done something properly.

'D'you need a hand with the food?' he asked Dutchy.

'We're all under control here,' said Titch. He handed Dutchy a tin of tuna and a packet of dehydrated noodles.

'Good, then,' said Aiden. 'I think I'll go and have a look at the creek.' He couldn't wait to take off his boots and plunge his feet in the cold water. His heels throbbed, and he wondered how he'd cope tomorrow.

'Careful!' called Steve. 'It flows fast in parts.'

'I'll only be gone a minute.'

He tried not to limp as he followed the call of the creek through the bracken. The sun had fallen below the treeline, and though his feet burned he shivered in the early winter evening.

The gurgle of water led him on, till he lost the smell of the campfire and bushes blotted his friends from view. He pushed through the bracken, lower now, and there it was, a clear, shallow stream snaking through the trees. Without untying the laces, he pulled off his boots and tossed them to the bank on the other side. He rolled up his jeans and eased his feet into the water. The cold burned his heels, but it was a healing sting, like digging his nails into an itch till it hurt. He waded to a rock in the centre of the stream and sat there, letting the water suck away his pain.

Whenever Aiden grew cross or cranky, his stepfather told him to 'go off and cool your heels.' He hardly ever raised his voice to Aiden, or showed any sign of temper. Well, Steve, thought Aiden, I'm cooling my heels!

He didn't want to think of home, yet it was never far from his mind. He wasn't sure he wanted to go back. How could he face Sabina and say he was sorry? What did Steve really think of him now? All Aiden wanted was for Steve to like him, but Sabina was *his* and she always stood between them.

The water swirled gently around his ankles. Above the rippling in the reeds, he heard the strum of a banjo. Just once. *Plonk*. Then again . . . *plonk*. Aiden hadn't seen anybody around. Yet someone was strumming further down the creek. *Plonk*. He stood up, and listened. The music came again, but nobody was there.

He waded to the other side and picked up his boots, then followed the bank downstream. Whoever was playing must have heard him, for the music stopped.

'Who's there?' he called. There was no answer. Only the gentle chuckle of the creek and drips falling from the trees.

It was Titch, having some sort of joke, he decided. He'd better be getting back. He pulled on his socks and eased his feet into the boots. Tomorrow, he'd put plaster on his heels. At least he'd remembered to bring that.

He began to wind his way through the bracken and back across the creek. The sun had slunk away, and the forest turned as grey as the evening sky. *Plonk*. His foot slipped, and for a moment he felt himself falling, falling into darkness. Night blotted out the forest and the sky, and everything around him was black. He reached for a scrubby branch and grabbed it. But the ground was firm under his feet and he wasn't falling at all.

He shook himself, and his head cleared. Every way he looked, wattle bushes and peppermints, rotting logs and leaf litter merged into the backdrop of giant trees. The forest was still there, but there was no murmur of creek.

'Yoohoo!' he called. The bush shifted into a deeper silence.

'Yoohoo! Can't anybody hear me?'

Nothing. The cries that came back to him were his own.

It would be dark soon and he couldn't stay here. Time was running out. He must find a path through the bushes, but he had no idea which way to turn. He listened, and still there was no sound of the creek. He must have come further than he'd realised.

From far in the distance he heard a long, low cry. Once, and then it died away. Could it be Dutchy? Dutchy might be worried about him. Aiden stood still, waiting and listening for another sign, but silence surrounded him. Then the cry came again, as if wrenched from the depths of the earth. It was a beckoning call, drawing him towards it, and it wasn't Dutchy.

A chill slithered around his shoulders. He didn't know that voice, yet it was calling to him. He couldn't see where it came from, but he felt the pull.

Had the voice cried '*come*'?

The third time it called, he knew he had to follow it. Aiden took a deep breath and plunged into the forest.

lost

HE KNEW HE was lost from the moment he stepped into the bushes. It was something Aiden thought would never happen to him. He began to run, trying to beat the night. He ran and ran, and his steps led him deeper into the woods.

The creatures of the forest were all out there. Yet he was alone. The voice he'd followed had abandoned him. Aiden couldn't think for the hammering in his brain. *Lost . . . lost . . . lost.*

Sabina and Steve and his mother's bumpy darning were pushed from his mind as he battled to find his way.

Chit-chit!

It was only a bird. A white-breasted robin clung to

the side of a wattle tree. It jerked its tail and flitted into the undergrowth. A twig flickered, but the bird had vanished.

When he stopped still, he could hear his heartbeat, pounding in his ears. Night was closing in, and he had no warm clothes, nothing to eat.

'Hoi!' he called. 'Hoi!' Surely, someone would come. There must be people somewhere. Hikers came from everywhere to walk in the forest. Yet Steve had told him you could spend days here and not see another soul. It sounded good at the time.

He knew it was wrong to keep walking. He should stay where he was, before he became more lost. But he couldn't rest among the clutter on the ground. Mouldering leaves and bark mounded around the trunks of the karris, reaching almost as high as his waist. There were spiders and other crawling things hiding among the litter. What else lay hidden in those murky bushes?

He couldn't stand up all night either, so he kept on walking in the darkness. A branch snapped close by, and before he could turn his head a group of kangaroos crashed through the trees in front of him. Three, four, five bounded across the giant screen and were gone, leaving a hollow echo of their intrusion.

Intruders? *I* am the intruder, he thought. I don't belong here at all. If I were a forest animal, I wouldn't feel cold like this. I'd know where to find something to eat. By now, Steve might be dishing out the meal. Aiden could see Dutchy lapping up the noodle stew. Good old Dutchy would make sure they put aside enough for Aiden.

He'd give anything to be out of the forest, to be back at the fire with Steve and Dutchy and Titch, or even safely at home. He must press on.

Tall trees surrounded him on all sides now. If he looked up, he could make out flecks of sky, steely and starless between the treetops. He could no longer see where he was treading. Twigs scratched his arms and leaves brushed against his face. The darkest room in their house was never as dark as this.

He had no idea how long he'd been walking. The others would be worried about him. He wondered whether they'd tell Mum he was missing. Missing? Come on, he told himself. You can get out of this.

Yet with each fumble forward, his courage drained away. The night was a black cat waiting to pounce. It was also many shadows of grey, painting pictures that deceived him. Wild patterns loomed about him, slipping from one form to another like ghostly sculptures. They stretched out long fingers, prickling his skin. On he staggered, through another thicket of melaleuca into another gully of bracken.

Oom! Oom! The call made him jump. He couldn't see where it came from. *Oom-oom-oom-oom!* He wished the noise would stop. He dared not walk one step that might take him closer to the thing that made it.

A twig cracked and a waft of air swept over his head. Aiden fell to his knees and shut his eyes, afraid to look. A tawny frogmouth, disturbed from its roost, flew silently from one tree to another. Aiden dug his nails into the damp earth, and crouched there, holding on, begging the ground to shelter him.

When he dared to look, it seemed that the earth was peeling away, opening slowly in front of him. He found himself staring into a deep hole. Down there, he could see only blackness. The cold washed over him, and made him shiver. 'Hold on,' he told himself. 'Don't fall in.' If the earth swallowed him now, no one would ever know. You could lie forever under the ground, un-discovered. The thought sent a tingle down his spine.

His knees shook as he pulled himself to his feet. He backed away, his heels groping in the dirt for traps that might lurk behind him.

When he looked down again, the ground lay solid in front of him. The hole had closed over, vanished . . . or perhaps it had never been there. The forest was playing tricks on his imagination.

Please, someone, come. 'Hoi! Hoi!' he called again, but his cries splintered like dried chips into the night.

His heels were throbbing. With each step, the pain stabbed so fiercely that he didn't feel the scratches on his face or the insect bites on his neck and hands. When he wiped his cheek with his finger, he felt the wetness, but didn't know it was blood. It was sweat, he thought, from fear rather than heat, for the night held the chill of winter.

A mist was seeping through the trees, enclosing him in its milkiness. The forest was a place of mystery, where people disappeared. 'I have disappeared from everyone but myself,' he said aloud, into the night.

Sabina once told him she'd rather drown than freeze to death in the snow. Aiden said he'd rather be shot. Sudden and quick. Being lost was neither sudden nor quick.

He shivered, squinting through the mist to find a way ahead. The forest was shifting, like scenery on a stage. He was stepping into another world, more bewildering than the dark hole he'd glimpsed before.

Through the misty veil, the grey-white trunks of karris glowed like stalagmites. Gleaming stalactites reached downwards, and water pooled around his boots.

The rain-soaked bushes were wet, glistening walls, closing in on him. Aiden stumbled. A clammy sweat stuck to his fingers. He knew there were caves in the area, famous caves with mirror-like lakes and lights reflecting stalactites and stalagmites like a castle of jewels. Somewhere, deep under the ground. But not here.

When he was little, Mum had taken him into the Lake Cave near Margaret River. He could still picture the clear, still water reflecting a wondrous world of stalactites, too beautiful to be real. When they'd come back into the air, he couldn't believe such a world existed.

Now he glimpsed it again, and he didn't want to be there. He trembled. Not tonight, not on my own. But when he blinked, the stalagmites and the water pool were gone, and the forest was visible through the mist as if they'd never been. I've started seeing things, he thought.

He held his watch to his face and saw it was past midnight. He'd been wandering for more than six hours. It shocked him to think how far he could have come in that time; how lost he might be now. He longed to lie down, but didn't dare. Spiders and other insects would crawl down his neck. Snakes not yet asleep could slither over him. He might never wake up.

Without looking where he was going, he began to run. He pushed branches out of his way, forcing a path through the undergrowth. Twigs sprung back at him, striking him across the shoulders and legs. Vines like tentacles grabbed him, holding him back. His arms flayed at them in panic, wrenching them away. He kept on running.

He wanted to cry out, but his voice stuck deep down in his stomach. The bush pressed in from all sides. A whippy branch smacked him across the cheek, jerking his head against the trunk of a tree.

The thud sounded inside his head, as if the forest were crashing down on him. Pain welled behind his eyes, turning everything black. Aiden slid to the ground, and then he felt nothing.

Was it minutes or hours later that he put a hand to his face and found himself lying on the forest floor? He didn't know what he was doing there in the dark, alone. Why did his head ache like this? He couldn't remember hurting himself, wherever he'd been.

What place was this, and how did he get here? He gazed into the forest, and the trees spun about him in circles. His head began to throb, and his mind was a jumble of questions. He uncurled and eased himself to his feet, and there, in the dimness he saw a glow.

He shuffled a few steps and stopped, gazing through the mist. The glow was a smoky blur burning steadily in the haze. Aiden pushed forward and dragged himself, faster now, towards the light.

found?

THE COTTAGE STOOD alone in a clearing near the edge of the forest. Rings of light seeped from its lamp, encircling the whole cottage in an eerie glimmer, as if it were suspended in the night.

Aiden parted the bushes and watched for a moment before he limped across the bare earth and knocked on the door.

Everything was still. Nobody came. The place is deserted, he thought. But someone had left the outside light on. He knocked again, and opened the door.

A light switched on inside the cottage and he heard the shuffle of footsteps from another room. A man in baggy pyjamas hunched towards him. His face was crushed with care and his sorry eyes blinked as if disturbed from a dream.

'I . . . er . . .' said Aiden.

The man gasped. He stepped forward and put both hands on Aiden's shoulders. 'You've come!' There was a sob in his voice.

He took Aiden's hand and led him further into the cottage. 'Mother, look!' he whispered, for he could hardly speak.

A woman stood, fiddling with the cord of her blue woollen dressing gown. She came towards him, slowly, in a kind of trance. Her lips trembled. 'Is . . . is it . . . ?'

A girl slipped into the room and stood behind the table. Her fingers gripped the back of a chair. She was like a wood nymph, suddenly there in her nightdress, slight and pale with chestnut hair waving about her shoulders. She stared at Aiden with questions in her eyes.

The air tingled with silence.

Then the woman kissed him.

Aiden couldn't think what to say. 'I'm . . . I'm . . . I can't remember, I've been lost . . . for so long.'

The woman watched him with a half-smile on her lips. There was something about her pale eyes. They didn't focus on him, but beyond him as if they could see into the distance. 'There, there,' she said. 'It's such a harsh place, out there.'

'I'm cold,' he mumbled.

The woman glanced at the man before she spoke. 'But you're safe now. We'll look after you.'

Aiden wanted to be looked after. The warmth of the small cottage soaked into his bones. These people didn't seem like strangers. Half of him felt he belonged here. The other half wanted to stay because he was so tired. I am not myself, he thought.

It was like being deep in a dream. You had to wait till you woke up, to find that you'd been dreaming. But he was awake. Tired, puzzled, but awake.

Words from a bushwalking book came back to him now. *Do not panic if you don't know where you are. You may be misplaced, but you are not lost.*

I am not lost, Aiden told himself. 'My head hurts,' he said.

'Let me look!' The woman parted his hair at the back. 'Oh, what a lump! How long have you had that?'

Aiden's eyes clouded. 'For a while, I think.'

Her eyes narrowed. 'I'm not so sure. The bruise hasn't come out yet. A little butter will help fix it.' She lifted the lid from a small crock and scooped out a fingerful of butter.

'Ouch!' said Aiden, as she rubbed it over the bump on his head. His hair would be all greasy now.

'There, there,' she murmured. 'And next we'll see to those scratches.' She took a torch and went out the back door. When she returned, she held a bunch of nasturtium leaves. She washed his face and hands with warm water and rubbed the sap of the leaves on his skin. 'There, you'll soon be your old self again.'

Aiden sat, gazing at the ceiling. He was going to be all right.

'When you get a cold, she'll make you eat the leaves,' said the girl.

Aiden grinned at her. He wouldn't be eating any leaves.

'Come,' said the woman, and pulled him to his feet. 'Your room is waiting.'

'*His* room?' said the girl.

'Ssh, Bryony!'

The man shook his head and smiled. 'I always knew he'd come.'

Aiden noticed the table was set, even though it was the middle of the night. There were four places, so they *were* expecting him.

The cottage had few rooms, and Aiden found his way around as if he'd always known it. The bedroom was small and cosy, like a ship's cabin. He felt comfortable here.

He opened a cupboard built into the wall. Two pairs of jeans hung from hangers, and the shelf was stacked with T-shirts, sweaters, socks and underpants. He pulled out a pair of jeans, but saw immediately that they were too small.

The T-shirts and sweaters were too small as well. But what about socks? Aiden pounced on a pair of black woollen ones, stretchy enough to fit him. He dragged off his boots and began to pull on a clean sock, then stopped. It was a warm fit, just like his own, yet it sent a shiver down his spine.

He padded into the main room and held the socks by the toes. 'Should I . . . is it all right if I wear these?'

'They're all yours,' said the man.

'But you need sleep now,' said the woman.

Aiden couldn't think of anything he wanted more. 'Thanks,' he murmured, and stumbled towards the bedroom.

'I'll brew you some camomile, so you have a good rest,' she said. 'Everything's going to be all right now.'

here we are again

HE LAY IN the narrow bunk and gazed at the timber beam close to his head. Outside, the wind swirled through the karri trees, whipping up a wail that could have been a child crying.

At last he could sleep. The bedclothes wrapped around him, and he felt at home. Yet there was a strangeness in the room, too, an emptiness he could feel, for something was lost. I am here, but I'm not here, he thought. Or was he just drifting off to sleep?

He must have slept, for whispers from the next room came suddenly, as if through an amplifier. The voices were hoarse, but clear.

'Could it be . . . ?

'Are you sure . . . do you really think . . . ?'

A muffled sound. A nod, perhaps.

'But how . . . ?'

'He's sent to us,' said the woman.

'That he is.'

Then, quickly, 'Bryony, go back to bed! It's only 5 am!'

Five o'clock. He *had* been asleep, though he felt as if his head had only just touched the pillow. He sank like a lead weight into the thin mattress, as if his body were pulling him down. Down, down, he didn't know where he was heading as he fell once again into a deep sleep.

He heard nothing and knew nothing more until daylight. Through the tiny peep of window he could see the sun slanting on karri trees at the edge of the forest.

He sat up in the bunk and his head nearly hit the timber ceiling. It was time to go. He had to leave, had to find . . . he didn't know what. He was looking for something, he was sure of that. If only he could remember . . .

He hadn't thrown off his blanket when the woman put her head around the door. 'Morning!'

'Hi,' he said.

She came into the room, dressed like nobody he

knew in neat woollen skirt, stockings and sturdy shoes. She smiled at him. 'I just wanted to be sure it was true.' Her eyes looked through him again.

'Eh?'

'That you're here.'

'Oh, I'm here.'

'How's your head this morning?'

He still felt the tightness of the lump. 'Getting better, I think.'

She drew open the small curtain. 'You like your room?'

He nodded.

'Nobody has touched a thing. We wouldn't let them.'

Aiden glanced about him, but there wasn't much in the room.

'Well, it's the same old breakfast,' she said. 'When you're ready.'

The steamy smell of warm milk drifted into the room. Breakfast here sounded good. He might stay to eat, and leave straight afterwards.

The girl was sitting down, sprinkling brown sugar over her porridge. Her hair was pulled into a ponytail, and her huge peacock-blue eyes gazed at him above the bowl.

29

'Hello,' he said, going towards the place set for him.

'But you're limping!' said the woman.

'It's only blisters. I'll be right.'

'Nonsense! We can fix them. There's herbs to be picked. Aloe vera's what we need.' She led him out the back door to a small, neat patch, where she had planted herbs. Nasturtiums spilled around the edges to the bricks below. Their orange and yellow flowers peeped through a cascade of soft green leaves.

'We had to go on living,' she said. 'And so I made a kitchen garden. I thought, one day I'll be needing aloe vera.' She bent and broke a piece from the thick, cactus-like leaf.

'Come inside. Now take off your boots and we'll rub on some of this sap.'

Aiden pulled off his boots and socks, as if it were natural to do as she told him. She leaned over him, and gasped at the sight of the red, broken skin. 'Ooh, they do look sore.' She opened the aloe leaf and placed a slice against each heel. 'Later, I'll be mixing you up a special potion. But for now, see how this feels.' She placed a wad of gauze against the leaves. 'And back with the socks. There now.'

Already, he felt the pain ebbing away. 'Thanks,' he said.

She nodded and smiled, pleased he hadn't forgotten his manners. 'There's breakfast to be eaten,' she called to her husband.

The girl sucked sugar from her fingers and with a finger still in her mouth ducked her head under the table, as if she were doing something wicked.

When her father came into the room, Aiden hardly recognised him from the night before. His back was straighter, as if the worries of the past had been lifted from his shoulders. He pulled a chair away from the table. 'Here we are and here we are and here we are again!' he said in a sing-song voice.

The girl dropped her spoon into the bowl. 'Oops!' She coughed, and leaned across to Aiden. 'It's just that he hasn't said that since the day . . .'

Aiden blinked at her. 'Since the day what?'

'Never mind,' she said, and went on eating.

'Bryony, get your father some fresh milk!' said the woman.

Aiden served himself a big bowl of porridge from the pot on the table. All this, he thought, and they don't even know who I am. 'My name is . . .' he said.

The woman smiled. 'I'm not surprised you've forgotten, after all you must have been through.'

The girl edged closer to him. '*What* happened?'

Aiden didn't know where to start. 'I got lost. Well, I *thought* I was lost till I saw your light.'

The woman nodded. 'We kept the light burning, Dugald. We never turned it off.'

'I'm not Dugald,' he said.

When the woman turned to him, he saw a tear drip from her left eye. It slithered down her cheek and plipped to the floor.

'I'm not,' he repeated. 'I . . . I don't think so.'

Two more tears fell from the same eye. She wiped them away with her finger. The other eye gazed at Aiden as if it were telling him something.

The man coughed. 'What do we care about names, eh?'

His wife gave a thin smile. 'We have no worries, then!'

Bryony pointed her spoon at Aiden. 'Tell us more,' she said.

'The ground opened up, and someone was calling me. I heard this sound, like someone playing a banjo. And I followed it.'

'Pobblebonk!' said the man. 'Always searching for the pobblebonk. Bryony, show him the banjo!'

She took a banjo from its hook on the wall, and plucked a string. *Plonk!*

It sounded just like the music in the creek.

'He made it,' said the girl. 'Like everything else in this place. He only finished it yesterday.'

'That I did,' said the man. 'Now, Bryony, put it back.'

The girl did as she was told.

The cottage walls glowed rich and red, making Aiden want to reach out and touch them.

'Just eat now,' said the woman. 'You can tell us all about it later.'

He was grateful not to have to talk. Yet all the time he ate, he could feel their eyes watching him, as if they would never let him go.

Bryony Fisk

EACH MOUTHFUL WARMED his stomach, and he felt he belonged here, in this cottage, with this family. They were drawing him in, as surely as if they'd wound a chain around him. Yet from somewhere in his memory, a voice called, and he knew he had to get away.

As soon as he finished breakfast, he took his plate to the sink. He needed to move from the table. The girl came across with the rest of the dishes and began to wash them.

'I'll help,' he said.

'That'd be a change!' she said and for the first time he saw a smile in her eyes.

'How old are you?' he asked.

She squinted at him, then grinned. 'I'm eleven now.'

'I guessed that.'

'And you're thirteen!'

'I must be.' He tried to laugh it off. There was so much he didn't understand about this family. He didn't even know their names, though he'd heard them call the girl Bryony. 'What's your other name?' he asked.

'Don't you know?' She pouted at him.

'Should I?'

'Don't you remember?'

'I don't know.'

'Fisk. Bryony Fisk.'

'How long have you been here, then?'

'In this cottage? Two years, but it seems like forever. They wouldn't leave till . . . They were waiting . . .'

'For me?' He reached out and touched her, and for a moment she could have been his sister. 'Tell me what happened.'

'Tell *you*! You should be telling us.'

'Tell me . . . about the two years.'

She screwed up her nose. 'There's nothing much to tell. Overnight, Mum and Dad changed. They don't think like other people any more. For a while, it was *so* boring. We seemed to sit all day, staring at each other. We were waiting, all the time waiting. They said,

"Dugald couldn't get lost in the forest—he knew every tree." People said, "Dugald's drowned—washed down the rapids into the river," But there was no . . . no sign, and Mum and Dad never believed it.'

A jolt of uncertainty whipped through him. Bryony was talking about someone else, but in some strange, unreal moments he felt she was speaking of him, too.

'Everything was kept the way it was left,' said Bryony. 'Mum wouldn't let me into the room. One day I asked if I could wear the old blue windcheater; Mum's face went rigid, like a slab of concrete. "It isn't yours!" After that, I didn't ask for anything that wasn't mine.'

'I'd give you my windcheater,' he said.

She tugged at his sleeve and laughed at him. 'When it's worn out?'

'What else would you like?'

Her face was puzzled. 'They never give me things, not even a book. But sometimes, if I ask, they say I can *take* something.'

Again he felt a bond with the girl he'd known for only a few hours. He wanted to know more about her. 'Didn't you ever go back to school?'

'When term started, I thought we'd go home, but we stayed. I wasn't the one who mattered. Mum taught me here for a while, and then she took me to the school through the trees. I never knew how long I'd stay. I felt as if I was only half there. But perhaps now we'll go back to town, and I can have friends again.'

'Doesn't your father go to work?'

She shook her head. 'He didn't ever go back to his city job. This was the place he'd always done his woodwork. He fiddled around like he did on all those school holidays, making things, polishing the walls. Every day the same thing . . . and waiting.'

For me, thought Aiden.

'Often he sat in a kind of trance,' said Bryony. Mum would stand over him and say, "There's work to be done. There's wood to be chopped, clothes to be washed." She had her ways of keeping going.'

'You poor thing,' said Aiden.

Her eyes flashed at him. 'Never! I'm not a poor thing.'

He winced, and drew away. 'Sorry.'

'Anyway, I'm glad you're here.'

a photograph

THE PARENTS SAT at the table, watching but not hearing. They smiled at one another, pleased that the children were getting along together.

'Things are going to be different from now on,' called Mrs Fisk. 'Tonight, we'll have a celebration. All your favourite food.'

'But I have to go.'

She jerked her head, and frowned at Aiden. 'Where?'

'I . . . I can't stay.'

The woman nodded to her husband. He cleared his throat and thought for a moment. 'You mustn't worry. We've fixed things up, haven't we, Mother?'

'You're with us now,' she said.

'But when . . . when can I go?'

'Everything is settled.' Her voice sliced through the room, cutting off his question. 'Dugald, you're home.'

Bryony was watching him with anxious eyes. She turned to her father, and Aiden heard her whisper. 'He isn't sure, can't you tell?'

Aiden rubbed his hand across his eyes. 'I . . . I need . . . I'm looking . . .'

'Yes,' said the woman. 'And we have ways of knowing.'

Aiden flopped on a chair and stared at the walls. They turned dark and slanted towards him. For the first time, he noticed the framed photograph on the dresser. He found himself drawn towards it, as if into a mirror. A boy's face stared out at him, a boy a bit younger than him with hair that stuck up in front, and lips pulled to one side in a half-smile.

'Dugald,' Bryony told him.

'Yes,' he said. There was that sound again! He'd heard the voice calling him before. A sudden chill gripped his shoulders, and he found himself staring into a narrow, dark tunnel. The room began to sway. He gripped the chair with both hands to stop himself from falling.

The opening led down to a black silence. The dampness crept right through his body. A dank smell hit his nostrils, and it was not altogether strange to him. His stomach knotted with panic. Will I ever get out . . . ?

'Are you all right?' When he looked up, the woman was standing over him. 'You're all pale.'

Aiden released his hold on the chair and saw that his knuckles were white, though his hands were wet with sweat.

Bryony stood, her head on one side, watching him. Her eyes never left his face.

He nodded to her. 'I'm fine.'

'You're with us now. You're safe,' said the woman.

'And there's nothing a good feed won't fix,' said Mr Fisk. 'Mother knows how to tempt us. What would you like her to cook tonight?'

'We don't have to ask.' The woman's eyes beamed at Aiden. 'Roast chicken and spaghetti, I know.'

He looked up. 'My favourite!' But I won't be here to eat it, he thought.

'And apple pudding without sultanas. I'll go into town this morning.'

'I'll come with you.' Mr Fisk stood and pushed his chair against the table. 'I'd like to sing out on the streets, that I would.'

'You stay here,' she whispered. 'Let's keep him to ourselves a bit longer.' She heaved a long sigh. 'I feel as if I've been holding my breath all this time, and I've only just started to breathe again.'

Mr Fisk rubbed his fingers over his mouth. 'That we have. But it's all in the past.'

She turned to Aiden. 'You get some rest, now.'

'I'll just stay here with Bryony,' he said.

'Of course,' said the man. 'It's been a long time.'

Bryony's eyes were watching him and they were singing, merry as a summer sky.

'Now, Bryony, don't you bother him,' said the woman as she picked up her basket.

'I won't get in the way, I promise.'

When they were alone, she gazed at Aiden. 'It feels funny, having you here. You *look* different, too. You had this bit of hair that stuck up in the air like a fountain. It isn't there any more.'

He ran his hand through his smooth, straight hair.

'And you curled your lip at me when we talked.'

'People change, I suppose.'

From the backyard came sounds of chiselling and grinding. 'Dad's started already,' said Bryony. 'He always said, "When Dugald comes back, I'll carve a special sculpture for the door."'

Aiden bit his lip, and listened as chips whittled from the wooden block. He was waiting for her to ask what happened, and where he'd been.

'Was it really awful? Were you hurt much?'

'Um . . . I can't remember. I don't think so.'

She stood up and danced around the table. 'It's like a miracle! Can you show me, one day, where you've been? I mean, where did you come from yesterday, out of the forest like that?'

'I told you, I was lost.'

'For two years! That's stupid!' Her ponytail bobbed as she tossed her head, and her green eyes blazed at him. He'd been wrong about her eyes when he thought they were blue, for they were green. Peacock-green.

'So where did you come from, really?'

He wished he could tell her, but he couldn't remember.

Bryony jutted her jaw at him. 'One day you'll tell us, and after that we can all be like we were before.'

She was as fragile and pretty as a doll, yet when she spoke she sounded much older and wiser. He smiled at her.

'It's not funny!'

'I'm not laughing.' He was thinking instead how good it felt, getting to know her. He liked her as a sister.

a map

AIDEN DIDN'T STOP to think any more. Or to wonder. A force was driving him. There was something he had to find.

He'd slip away now, before Mrs Fisk came back from town.

He went to the bedroom to collect his jacket. His old football socks hung over the side of the bunk. The new stitching stood out against the faded section on the heels. He stared as if he hardly recognised them, and tossed them to the floor.

Before he left, he needed to check out his room. He opened a drawer in the wall cupboard, where Dugald kept his special things. It stuck around the edges, as if it hadn't been opened for a long time.

Aiden was delving into places where no one had been since Dugald left. The mess inside was not new to him.

He rummaged through an assortment of blunt pencils, an insect trap, woolly tennis ball, the first *Harry Potter*, a torch and spare batteries, a book on caving, scrappy bits of paper and something that looked like a finger-bone. When he picked it up, it was cold and stiff against his skin.

He dropped it quickly and heard the clink as the tip broke off. It was not a bone, but some sort of crystal, rather like a shred of coral washed smooth by the sea. He laid the two pieces carefully back in the drawer.

He was after something else, something more important. It had to be there. He ran his fingers around the drawer, where sheets of paper had been pushed to the back, hidden. Aiden fished out a piece and unfolded the page. The map.

Here it was, a rough sketch with a track leading from the cottage through the forest. Yes, this was the way. He sat down on the bunk to study the page.

The track started at a spot marked and crossed the clearing into the forest. Past the Crooked Tree, it skirted a small camp called Ringneck Roost, then veered away from the Mudslide and turned right through the Orchid Patch.

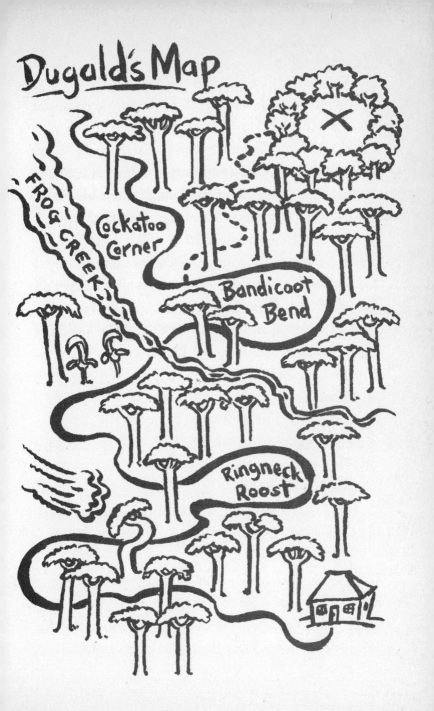

Aiden traced the creek with his finger, till it crossed the path that circled Bandicoot Bend on the way to Cockatoo Corner. Another track veered towards Waterbush Gully, just a series of dots snaking between the trees. He felt a tingle of excitement when his finger reached the place marked **X**. It lay deep in the forest, and no one else knew about it.

He tucked the map into his jacket pocket and closed the drawer. He could slip away now, while Bryony and her father were in the backyard.

Just as he touched the front doorknob, he heard the clink of the kitchen door, and Bryony's voice calling to him. 'Where are you going?'

'Where?'

'Yes, silly!'

'For a walk.'

'Then I'll come.'

'No, you can't.'

Her face crumpled in shock. 'I thought you were nicer. Why can't I come?'

'I have to go alone.'

She wrinkled her nose at him. 'Why do you have secrets?'

He couldn't explain, even to himself. And when he saw the plea in her blue-green eyes, he began to waver.

She didn't get much of a go in this house. She was an outsider within the family.

It hurt him to say it. 'I'm sorry. You can't come today.' He pushed the door open and ran across the clearing before he could change his mind.

The wind had dropped, and a hush descended on the forest, as if all the wildlife had slipped into a mid-morning sleep.

Aiden took a narrow track, where fallen leaves had packed into a damp, dark carpet. He could feel its coolness through his boots. The gel was comforting on his heels, and helped him to walk without limping.

He stopped to look up, and the sky was a long way above. A speckled black cloud whirled around the treetops. It could have been a plague of insects.

'Lorikeets!' said a voice beside him. Her footsteps were so soft on the ground that he hadn't heard a twig snap.

He had no time to put the map back in his pocket. 'Bryony, what are you doing here?'

'I came to see the lorikeets!' she said, and peered to see if he was angry.

'Birds look so small from a distance,' he said.

'And we look like possums to them.'

He couldn't be cross with her.

'I didn't want you to get lost again,' she said. 'And what would I have told them, that I'd let you go?'

'I'm sorry, then.'

'What's that in your hand?'

The map was his secret. He didn't want to show her. 'It's . . . er . . . a drawing.'

She grabbed it from his fingers. 'Oh, you've got the map. I *knew* there was a map!' She unfolded it and jabbed her finger on the Orchid Patch. 'That's where we found the clump of helmet orchids, I remember! And here's where we had the picnic, beside the Crooked Tree, where I got bitten by the ant.' She turned to him. 'So where are we going now?'

He pointed to the spot marked **X**. 'Do you know this?'

She peered at the paper. 'Another no-name place. You tell *me*.'

'Maybe.'

'Why won't you tell me things?'

'I *am* telling you, aren't I! I'm showing you the map.'

'Then let's follow it,' she said. 'Come on, lead the way!'

The track wound deeper into the forest. Aiden stared into the distance, watching and listening.

Bryony grasped his hand and pulled him on. 'Have you forgotten the way?' She skipped ahead of him as if she belonged among the trees. As she flitted between shadows, the stillness and silence were eerie.

She danced in a circle around a tree with a trunk twisted into a question mark. Here was the Crooked Tree, so different from all the tall, straight karris of the forest.

'If we take this fork, we can walk through the Orchid Patch to the creek,' she said. 'Hurry up, we might hear the pobblebonk again.'

Through the thickets of melaleuca and acacia, he heard the sound of running water. The track came out at a wide section of the creek, where a fallen tree formed a rough, narrow bridge.

'That's new!' said Bryony. 'It must have come down in the last storms.'

She stepped on to the log and edged forward, holding out her arms for balance.

While her back was turned, Aiden ran his fingers through his hair and messed it up, leaving a few strands sticking up in front. He crept on the log behind her, and fixed his lips into a thin smile, with his mouth curled on one side. 'Boo!'

She turned to face him and flung her arms in the air, tilting one way and then the other before she overbalanced into the water.

For a moment, he laughed. Then he saw her face, twisted in shock and in pain. She stood, clinging to the log with water swirling around her knees. Her eyes bored into him.

'I'm sorry. Are you hurt?'

'It *is* you!'

'It was a joke.'

'Very funny! Now I've hurt my ankle.'

Aiden jumped into the creek. 'I'll get you out. Don't worry.' Now, look what he'd done! 'How bad is it?' he asked.

When she tried to walk away, he saw tears squeeze from her eyes. He touched her arm. 'Come and sit here for a minute, and see how it feels.'

He helped her to a low, flat rock near the fallen tree. It was only a few metres to the other side, but the creek bed was uneven and slippery. They sat together on the rock with their feet in the water. Only then did he realise they both had their boots on.

She stared at him. 'It *is* you, isn't it?'

'Of course it's me, Dugald, who else?'

'For a while, I never really believed it, but now I know.'

'Look, I didn't mean to frighten you.'

'I know, you thought it was funny, looking like you

used to be. I like you better the way you are now.'

He knew she couldn't go any further with her swollen ankle. He'd have to help her home. 'Do you think you can walk?' he asked.

'I'll try.'

'Come on, then, let's go.' He held her hand as they waded back to the bank. She brushed him away, but he saw her wince when she put her foot to the ground.

'Here, lean on me,' he said.

They stumbled along the track together. Water squelched inside their boots, and their wet jeans were cold against their legs.

'We'll be in trouble with Mum and Dad,' she said.

The forest was still half-asleep, so the crackle of bushes made him stop. His fingernails dug into Bryony's arm. 'What's that?'

She looked around. 'Nothing.'

He listened, holding his breath, waiting for another sign. Through the trees, he saw a flash of khaki, and a flickering of leaves in the undergrowth.

He dragged Bryony to the side of the track and pushed her into a thicket of wattle bushes.

She opened her mouth to complain, but he clapped his hand over her lips. 'Ssh!' he whispered. 'Someone's coming!'

She stared at him as if he were a complete stranger. He felt a stranger to himself, too. Something inside him had cried out, 'Hide!' He held Bryony back as the rustle of footsteps came closer. The ranger walked by with a boy about Aiden's age. The boy had a friendly, pudding face, and Aiden thought he'd like him if he knew him.

He and Bryony lay flat among the bushes, hardly breathing, till they had passed. He breathed out at last, and peeped through the bushes. 'They've gone.'

Bryony sat up and frowned at him. 'What's going on?'

'I . . . They're looking for me.'

'Don't be stupid! They gave up ages ago.' Her face was wreathed in the leaves of their hideout, with the shadows reflected in her eyes. 'Is something the matter?'

'Forget it,' he said.

'Me? Forget! How can you say that?'

'Just let me do things my own way.'

She hung her head. 'I thought you'd changed, but you haven't. You're still running away.'

'I never did.'

'Then why did you go off in the middle of the night like that?'

'I never.'

She crashed her fist into the ground. 'Stop saying

never! You *did!* And not just that time, either.'

He grinned at her. He liked her when she was cross. She treated him as someone worth arguing with. And it was true, there were things he hadn't told her. Some things he couldn't explain, not yet.

He shrugged, and pulled her to her feet. 'Come on, we're going home now.'

Bryony knows

THE COTTAGE DOOR was open, and they could hear raised voices.

'I *told* you!' shouted the woman. 'How could you let him go?'

The man mumbled as words clogged in his throat. 'I trusted them, Mother. Besides, the sculpture was taking shape . . .'

'We're here!' called Bryony.

Mrs Fisk came to the door. She threw out her arms in welcome, and glanced back over her shoulder. 'I told him not to worry. Come along now, I've been baking.'

Bryony flopped into the closest chair. 'She fell over,' said Aiden. 'Could you put something on her ankle?'

Mrs Fisk pointed to their feet. 'Just look at your shoes! What have you been doing?'

'We went for a walk,' said Bryony.

Her mother clicked her tongue. 'There's places for walking and there's places for swimming.'

Bryony hunched her shoulders and cupped one hand over her mouth, but Aiden could see from her eyes that she was laughing.

'So?' said her father.

'We fell in,' said Bryony.

He jabbed his finger in the air and pointed at her. 'I never want to hear that again!'

'Sorry,' she said meekly.

Aiden bent down and unlaced Bryony's boots. She pulled off her socks to see that her right ankle was already puffy.

Mrs Fisk was busy, peeling apples for the pudding.

'Aren't you going to put something on Bryony's ankle?' asked Aiden.

She wiped her hands on a towel and walked across to her daughter. 'I suppose it does need something.'

'I'll get it,' he said. 'What do you want?'

'A few daisy leaves will fix it.'

'Um . . . which is the daisy?'

The woman put a hand on his arm. 'Don't you worry, I'll get it.' She came back with a spray of small white daisies, and wrapped the leaves around Bryony's ankle. 'Daisy,' she murmured. 'Day's eye.'

'Eh?' said Aiden.

'It opens its petals in the morning light.' Her own eyes were veiled, like a cloudy dawn. 'Day's eye, to fix a sprain.'

Aiden wanted to take off his boots too, but he didn't have other shoes to fit. Mrs Fisk stood back and shook her head at him. 'In all the excitement, we forgot about clothes for you.'

'I'll be right,' he said.

She slapped her hands together, up and down like a cymbal player, and turned to the wood stove. 'Well now, there's work to be done, food to be cooked. Special food!'

'Do you need any help?' asked Aiden.

'You sit down there and talk to Bryony,' she replied. 'I've got plenty of time.'

'We all have plenty of time,' said Mr Fisk, and his smile reached every corner of the room. 'That we do now.'

Aiden pulled a chair beside Bryony. 'You can't sit here in soggy boots,' she said.

He cocked his head towards the stove, where

Mr Fisk was helping his wife with the cooking. 'Don't they get snitchy about bare feet?'

'You didn't worry about that before.'

'Okay, I'll put them outside to dry.' He squished out the back door and laid his boots and socks in the sun. He could use some new socks, or he'd have to wear those old ones he'd left on the bedroom floor.

His wrinkled, white feet didn't look like his own. For a moment, he imagined how a body might look after days or weeks in the water. Quickly, he pushed the picture from his mind.

'Spooky toes!' said Bryony when he came back. 'You look like a ghost.'

He shook himself and tried to smile. 'I was just thinking.'

'Something interesting?'

'About socks.'

'Socks!' She tossed her head and gave a little snort. 'How boring!'

True, socks were boring. His shoulders began to shake and he laughed until his eyes watered.

'That's more like it,' she said.

'Like what?'

'The real Dugald. When you laughed, tears always ran down your cheeks.'

This sister knew so much about him, and remembered so much. And sometimes she seemed to read his thoughts.

'You were always smarter than me, Dugald,' she said. 'You were going places.'

'D'you reckon?'

'Mum and Dad always knew you were clever. They reckoned you'd be an explorer. They said one day there'd be a mountain somewhere called Dugald's Peak.'

Aiden touched his pocket to feel the map. 'I was looking for something.'

'Like what?'

He grinned at her. 'Maybe the pobblebonk!'

'Ha! Ha! What's new about frogs? You had to be first with everything. You wanted something bigger than that.' She tilted her head to face Aiden. 'I knew you'd gone out that last night. I heard you leave. I was scared to go to sleep in case I woke up to find you'd put a spider in my bed. But when it was the middle of the night and still you hadn't come back, I got worried.'

'Things always seem worse in the night.'

'I never thought you wouldn't come back. Truly, I didn't. Even though you were only eleven, you knew the forest. But it rained. It rained and rained.' She nodded towards the house. 'I knew you were out there, but they didn't. I didn't want to get you into trouble, so I didn't wake them. I waited too long. By morning, it was too late.'

'It wasn't your fault.'

'I never told them I'd known you were out there in the night. The days passed, and the forest was full of searchers. They dragged the river, and kept bringing us things that might have been yours . . . a jacket, a wallet, gold chain, a shoe and even old food packets. Nothing belonged to us. We went on, wanting to believe you hadn't really gone. Mum and Dad would never give up.'

He watched her face as she relived the past two years.

'So you see,' she went on, 'I'm happy you're back, and that you're you, because I don't feel so bad any more.' Her eyes brightened. 'And maybe, now, soon, we can go back to town and I can have friends again.'

Aiden wriggled on the chair, as if the map was burning a hole in his pocket. 'Maybe, soon . . .' He jumped up and walked to the window. 'Yes, maybe.'

He still had something to do.

Dugald's things

'HERE WE ARE and here we are and here we are again,' chanted the man when they sat down to dinner.

It was supposed to be a celebration, but Aiden couldn't sit still. The pull of the forest grew stronger as dusk turned to dark. This was the night he must go.

'Thank you, it was very nice,' he said when he'd finished the apple pudding. It was too polite to be the voice of anybody's son.

'Bryony will do the dishes if you want to go to bed,' said Mrs Fisk.

'I'll help,' he said, though he couldn't wait to escape.

As soon as he and Bryony had finished the washing-up, he said he'd like an early night. There were a few things in his room he needed to check more closely.

When he opened the drawer, he picked up the broken finger-bone and ran his fingers over the smooth surfaces, knowing this was a piece of stalactite, taken from a cave. The Fisks believed Dugald would be an explorer and scale high peaks, but he was going down, not up. He was an underground climber.

They'd never seen his diary, or they would have known. He'd inserted a page inside the book on caving. Now, Aiden opened the book at pages 6–7, and sat on the bunk to read.

Australia's south-west from Cape Naturaliste to Cape Leeuwin is laced with limestone caves formed over millions of years. The next sentence had been underlined in ink: *There are at least 300 known caves in the area, but very few have been thoroughly explored.*

And written in the margin was: **301**

Four, all of spectacular beauty, are open to the public.

Vertical passages called sink or swallow holes lead down from ground level. Hundreds of tunnels run for kilometres underground, and many of these may open into huge chambers or caves.

Caving can be dangerous. Cavers must be fitted out with headlamps and equipment for underground rock climbing.

They may come across ice-cold rivers and cliffs to be scaled like mountains. Many passages are only just wide enough for cavers to wriggle through. At times, there is total darkness.

Aiden felt the cold in his bones. Tonight, he would complete what he set out to do. He unfolded the sheet of paper torn from the diary and read Dugald's handwriting.

Saturday 17th April: School goes back on Monday, so I only have today. Mum and Dad say I'll climb great heights. Ha! I'm going the other way. I'm not waiting till I'm old, either.

Tonight I found out you can see lightning with your eyes shut. I wish the rain would stop. I'll need a better torch. When they're all asleep, I'll borrow Dad's. He won't ever know.

We had my favourite food tonight—chicken and spag and then Mum's apple thing without sultanas.

Aiden gulped. The taste of dinner was still in his mouth.

cry of the karri

NOW CAME THE waiting time, waiting for the others to go to sleep. Aiden lay on his bunk, and felt himself pulling away from the cottage and from the family. Sometimes, it seemed, further even from himself. Only the forest was real.

Again and again, he went over things in his mind. He memorised the map till every detail stood out in his head. Dugald had taken his father's torch. He'd have to do the same tonight. This time, he'd take the chisel, too.

A rap on the cottage door jolted him from his plans. He yanked the blanket over himself as he heard the door creak open.

'Hello, Bert,' said Mr Fisk.

'I'm sorry to bother you,' said a man's voice. 'I know how hard this will be for you, but I'm afraid another boy has gone missing. You haven't seen anything, have you?'

This must be the ranger. Aiden held the blanket under his chin and strained to listen. The Fisks' replies were muffled. Someone coughed.

'Just checking,' said the man. 'It seems there might have been some problem, so if you see the boy at all, this is important. There's a message to be read to him, something from his sister. You could tell him that.'

'That I will,' said Mr Fisk.

What sister? thought Aiden. He didn't need any messages.

'Thank you, I know you'll contact us if you come upon anything.' The door closed, and the ranger's footsteps faded back into the night.

The Fisks turned off all the lights. There was no sound from Bryony's room.

They're still looking, thought Aiden. But they won't stop me. He knew with certainty now that he had little time left.

When the cottage was quiet, he slid from his bunk. He dared not risk walking through the house and out the creaky front door. His window was slightly ajar, so he eased it open and climbed to the ground.

In darkness, he crept to the back of the cottage, where he knew he'd find the tools. Inside the small, open shed, everything had its place. It was easy to put his hand on the chisel. He slipped it into his jacket pocket. An almost-new torch stood on the top shelf, beside candles and furniture wax. It was just what he needed.

So far, so good. He crossed the clearing and wove his way through the trees, afraid to use torchlight until he was well away from the cottage. The forest was a big, black world, but he knew where he was going.

Past the Crooked Tree, he switched on the torch to check the map. He felt he hardly needed it. He knew the route by heart, and was driven along it as surely as night was drawing towards the dawn.

The torch's beam made the world shrink around him, enclosing him in a small circle of light. The closest karri trunks shone like pillars of stone. Keep walking, he told himself. This is the way.

Bushes clustered ahead like a dark curtain. The ground shifted and he knew something was there. He moved the torch and captured two shining eyes in its beam. They stared, burning into him. He gripped the torch in stiff fingers. 'Keep calm,' he mumbled. 'Don't say a word.'

Seconds passed while he listened to the sound of his

own breathing. His eyes began to adjust to the light, and around the glowing eyes he made out the shape of an animal. It was almost the size of a cat, with a tail like a rat, but it wasn't a rat. Brush-tail Possums' eyes glowed orange-red in the night, so it wasn't a brush-tail, either. It might be a Southern Brown Bandicoot, and he knew it wouldn't hurt him.

He lowered the torch back to the muddy track. On a bend he recognised a slash of orange, low on a karri trunk, and knew he was heading for the Orchid Patch and then the creek.

There, like a dark shadow across the water, lay the log Bryony had fallen from this morning. He wondered whether she'd heard the ranger at the door. There hadn't been a sound from her bedroom.

He edged across the log and headed into the bush. The track twined between bracken, leading him deeper into the forest. Aiden stumbled on past Bandicoot Bend and stopped when he came to a fork in the path. A track on the right appeared to lead nowhere, but the way was clear inside his head. This was a place hikers didn't know about, a place where no one would follow him.

Sticks attacked him from all sides, like an army trying to hold him back. He had to go on.

A dark barricade of bushes loomed in front of him.

He thrust out a foot to force an opening. The sharp crack of twigs made him jump, but when he stood still the forest fell silent again.

He reached into his jacket for the map, but the pocket was empty. It wasn't in his jeans pocket either. He must have dropped it somewhere along the track. It was too late now to go back. He'd have to rely on his memory.

Even without the map, he knew he was knocking on the door of Waterbush Gully. The bushes had grown sturdy and thick, forming an unbroken ring around the mysterious **X**. There was no opening in the circle. Like a solid wall, the bushes protected Dugald's secret.

It was a barrier he must cross. Tonight. He fended sticks and leaves from his face and shouldered his way into the thicket. There seemed no end to the bushes, which stretched as far as he could see. Twigs scratched his face as he edged deeper into the gully. The slope was gentle, taking him down through a tangle of undergrowth. He knew where it was leading.

Time meant nothing now. The darkest dark told him it was still night. But then at last, his torch lit up a break in the bushes. Aiden stood on the edge of a crater as wide as a basketball court, overgrown with small shrubs and bracken. He flicked the torch around the fringes, where giant karris towered like guardians of the grotto. A breeze stirred now, sending a soft moan through the branches.

This was where he must go. Could there be another Lake or Jewel Cave under his feet?

The torch threw a green gloss over ferns that reached to his waist. Their fronds were damp and prickly. The mossy scent of earth hung in the air.

Aiden trod warily, careful not to slip on ground he could smell but not see. He clung to bracken stalks to keep his balance on the slope, which grew steeper as he went down.

When he reached the bottom, he looked up. Karri trees formed a ceiling above his head. The branches swirled, and their wailing was like the cries of a child, far away, nowhere in sight.

in the dark

IT WAS LIKE wandering inside a giant basin. Aiden scrambled around the bottom, groping against the earthen walls, feeling his way in the darkness. Behind a curtain of ferns, water dripped in glistening strands. He ran his hand through the wet and across the soft limestone wall till his fingers dipped into a crack.

He stopped. A charge of excitement whipped through his chest. A deep split reached back into the rock as far as he could see. Here it was, his cave!

Aiden took a deep breath before he entered. But something was wrong. A giant boulder blocked the opening.

When, and how, had this happened? He pushed

against the boulder, but it didn't budge. It hadn't been moved for a long time. He thrust his foot into the opening, and that was as far as he could go. The gap wasn't wide enough for even the skinniest child to enter. Only a snake could wriggle through there.

Disappointment dulled his senses. This was no longer the way into the cave. He'd have to find another entrance.

The only other way was from the top. A passage from above would be harder to find, and more dangerous, but now he had no choice. He must search for one of those sink or swallow holes he'd read about.

Knowing he must hurry, he felt his way up the slope, out of the green basin. Fern fronds swished against his legs and karri trees whined above him. Their cries were a warning. He was walking into danger. If there were holes leading down, this was treacherous country. One false step and he may never be heard of again. But there was no giving up. Nothing could stop him now.

Tunnels run underground for kilometres, the book said. A sink hole leading to the cave could be in a part of the forest a day's trek from here. But his cave was here, under his feet. This was where he had to start.

He reached the rim of the crater and took the first

fumbling step on ground that might hide the underground cavern.

It would be safer to crawl on his stomach, feeling the earth around him, but the idea gave him the shivers. Tiny, mouse-like mardos scampered among litter on the forest floor. He shone his torch on his boots and shuffled one way from the edge of the crater through the scrub to the wall of bushes, then back the other way. A search like this could take weeks. Don't think like that, he told himself. I have to find it.

One foot after the other, eyes fixed on every leaf, every blade of grass, steadying the torch, hoping the batteries would last . . . one foot after . . . He stopped. The toe of his boot rested a shoestring away from a hole in the ground.

He dropped to his hands and knees and shone the torch down the hole. A narrow shaft ran like a chimney, deep into the earth. Could it be, he'd found a sink hole? If it was what the book called a passage, it must lead somewhere. Two or three metres below the surface, a ledge protruded into the shaft. His beam didn't carry to the bottom, which seemed to open into wider darkness. A tunnel! A tunnel that would lead him to a world of jewelled stalactites and stalagmites. To 301.

Aiden sat back on his ankles. Though karri trees

soared above him, for a moment he sensed that he was sitting on top of the world. There was another world down there, and he wasn't afraid of entering it.

The hole was big enough to climb through, and the ledge not too far from the surface. Grasping bushes on the edge of the hole, he eased himself, feet first, into the shaft. There was no other way but to drop to the ledge. He pressed his back against the wall to slow his fall, and let go of the bushes. Whoosh! In an instant he slid to the ledge.

He twisted his head to inspect the scabby walls. A clump of small stalactites hung from a niche near his shoulder. They were grubby with dust and stunted, only a hint of the real show under there. Aiden shifted his feet, trying to focus the torch on the passage below. The rock cracked under his boot, and with a grinding crunch the ledge broke away from the wall. He dropped the torch and grabbed at the rock, scraping his fingers as he slipped down, down, he didn't know how far till he crashed on rocks at the bottom.

Aiden uncurled slowly and tried to stand up. His head hurt. It was dark, and he was cold. A clammy smell filled his nostrils. He put out his hand, and the floor was damp. His legs shook as he stumbled to his feet and looked around him.

A shock of fear, like a pain, ripped through his chest. He didn't know this place, or how he'd come to be here. A knifelike pain stabbed his shoulder. I must have fallen over, he thought. If anyone had been looking, he would have jumped straight to his feet. I'm all right! he'd say, before he really knew. But he was alone. And he *was* all right. If only he knew where he was.

He stood unsteadily and gazed above his head to a pale circle of light. He shuddered. That's how he came to be here! He'd fallen down the hole. How? Why?

And slowly, as if a series of locked doors opened inside his head, he began to remember. A picture of Bryony flashed before him, a girl who was like a sister, but his sister's name was Sabina. One by one the doors opened, and he knew he'd come to the forest with Steve and his friends, and he'd become lost.

There was someone called Dugald, who'd lent him his things. No, that wasn't right. He didn't know Dugald at all. He'd only heard about him, and read one of his books. About caves. The dank walls about him told him that's where he was now. In a cave.

Dugald hadn't been seen for two years, yet it was Dugald who'd led him here.

How could this have happened? Where have I been since I left Steve and the others? *Who* have I been? He put his hands in front of his face and stared at his fingers. *His* hands, *his* fingers. 'I am Aiden,' he said aloud. 'I'm Aiden, and I have to get out of here.'

He fumbled in the darkness till his boot struck something on the ground. A torch lay close to where he'd fallen. It wasn't his torch. Inside his head, another door opened. 'I think I pinched it,' he mumbled. He picked it up and held it unsteadily, shining the beam towards the roof. Far above his head, the hole he'd fallen through blinked down on him like an eye, and almost as small. He knew he wouldn't get out the way he'd come in.

The cavern wasn't much bigger than a four-man tent, and a bit like an animal's lair. A tunnel led off on one side. If he was to escape, he had no choice but to follow it. He must find a way out, for his own sake and for Dugald's, because he had the feeling Dugald had been here before him.

Dugald

HE DIDN'T KNOW how long he'd been in the dark. Not being able to see, not knowing what lay ahead. But he had to save the torch batteries.

His mind wriggled with spiders and snakes and passages that led to dead ends. He dragged himself along the tunnel on his stomach, edging further into blackness.

It must lead somewhere. He had no idea how far he'd have to crawl to find out. The longer he went on, the further he travelled from the sink hole. But there was no turning back. It was forward or nothing.

His shoulder jolted with every movement and the damp soaked through to his skin. He longed to switch on the torch, but had to tough it out in the dark. The batteries might have to last days while he found a way out.

The mouldering ceiling pressed down on him, crushing the air from his lungs. The tunnel narrowed with every breath. What if he became stuck? He wanted to scream, but his throat was clogged, and what was the use? No one could help him now. Only himself. He couldn't give up.

The stink of stale water and crumbling rock filled his nostrils. *Malodorous*. The word oozed into his mind from the fetid air that clung to him. I don't say things like that, he thought. *Malodorous?* The place was just plain smelly.

But the word wouldn't go away. It twisted and turned inside him and shouted in his ear like a pop tune he'd tired of long before.

They say people go mad underground. They see things and dream things, and lose their reasoning. That's what's happening to me, thought Aiden. *Malodorous*. When he saw a half-light in the tunnel ahead, he felt he was dreaming. He grovelled on the damp, rocky floor, urging himself onward, forward towards that thin slit of light.

The air ahead hung in a thick pall, fading to pale like moments before morning. He knew he wasn't hallucinating. His breath came faster and his body moved smoothly along the tunnel. No headache or injured shoulder could stop him now. There was another sink hole ahead, and perhaps a way to the top.

As he came closer to the light, the tunnel opened into a small cavern, uneven in shape and twice as big as the cave below the first sink hole. On the other side another tunnel ran off into darkness. Aiden stopped under the shaft of light and raised his head. The steep, high passage narrowed till the opening appeared no bigger than a cricket ball. He was deeper down, far deeper, than he'd imagined.

He dragged himself to his knees and breathed deeply, now he had room to move. His chest ached. His legs shook in the damp jeans that clung to his skin. He stood up, as if that would bring him closer to the top, but saw that without ropes there was no way out from here.

Aiden stumbled into a corner to rest, and to work out what to do. Like stumpy icicles, a few stalactites hung down from the roof that almost brushed his head. He sat on the slimy floor and stared into the tunnel on the other side. He'd have to worm his way along that tunnel. It was his only chance.

Right now, he didn't feel like going anywhere. His body ached all over, and his mouth was dry and furry. His eyes gazed ahead, seeing and not seeing, until a small object came into focus just inside the mouth of the tunnel. It was, perhaps, a fragment of stalactite like the piece Dugald had souvenired from the cave.

Aiden stumbled across and bent to touch it. He gasped and pulled away, for this wasn't any broken stalactite. It was a bone, a real finger-bone, and it was part of a hand.

He shivered as he peered more closely at his discovery. The bony finger beckoned, like a command, from its blackened claw. Aiden's mouth hung open as he backed away. His feet tripped on the uneven floor. Struggling for breath, he picked up the torch and forced himself back to the shrivelled hand. He kneeled beside it and shone the torch into the tunnel. And there he saw the frayed sleeve of a jacket . . . and more bones . . . another skeletal hand, a hunched shape surprisingly small, and a head, its collapsed face as blackened as the hands.

Aiden switched off the torch. His chest was heaving, but he couldn't breathe. A cold sickness seeped through his body, for he knew who he had found.

Dugald's secret

DUGALD HADN'T MADE it, so how could he? Aiden flopped in a corner of the cavern to take in what he'd discovered. He wanted to run, but he had nowhere to go. Nowhere, except along the tunnel where Dugald lay. The horror of pushing past that body brought a sickening taste back to his mouth. But he had to try.

'You were trapped by the rain, Dugald,' he said. 'You didn't fall in here, like I did. The rock fell across the entrance that night, and trapped you. Now we're both here, and it's all up to me.'

Aiden picked up his torch and crawled into the tunnel. The musty smell of a woodpile filled his nostrils.

'I won't hurt you, Dugald,' he said. He must not crush or disturb anything.

The seam of Dugald's jacket stood out against the crumbling fabric. Aiden wondered why he noticed such a thing. He swallowed hard, and grovelling on his stomach edged gently past the shrunken body.

Ahead, the tunnel narrowed and he could see nothing without his torch. His beam picked up Dugald's rusting torch and then, only a few metres further on, a rock wall that blocked the way. With a sinking feeling in his chest, Aiden pushed towards it. While he had the strength to crawl, he had to go on. Forward, not back.

His arms reached out as he dragged himself on, bit by bit, inching towards a solid rock wall. This was the end of the tunnel.

To give in now would be easy. He could lie his head on the wet rock and never raise it again. Yet he couldn't let Dugald down. He had to go on; to *try* to go on.

When he shuffled to one side, he felt a jab to his rib and remembered there was something in his pocket. It was a chisel. He wondered why he had one with him, but it was like a gift now, in the dark tunnel. He fumbled to pull it from his pocket and drove it into the rock in front of him. A few soft chips broke away, but the wall remained as solid as before.

'Keep going,' he told himself. He cracked the chisel into the rock. Again and again. Each blow sent more specks showering around his head. Thwack crash jab . . . phew! Sweat dripped from his face. His fingers stung from the grip on the handle. He took a sharp breath and began again. Thwack crash jab. Jab jab jab. And again. He chiselled till a small crack opened in the rock. He chiselled till the crack widened to a split.

He had to rest a moment, but only for a moment. Jab jab jab. He was making a dent in the rock. The split was deepening. A hollow sound gave him hope that there was another side to the wall. Somewhere beyond this dark passage, could there be an escape?

A rank smell stuck in his nostrils. He felt his air was almost at an end. He was wedged in the tunnel between Dugald and the wall. Yet he was making a dent. There was some hope left.

Twack crash jab. On and on, again and again, till the chisel slipped in his fingers, and the tip hovered, suddenly free. He'd broken through!

Aiden pressed his eye against the small peephole, but everything was black. He couldn't see a thing. He needed light to find what lay on the other side of the wall.

Once again, he set to work with the chisel. He ground and scraped, chiselling away at the rock till he

could shine the torch through the hole. With his eye
close to the torch-face, he flicked on the switch.

Aiden gasped. He found himself gazing into another
world, a wonderland of ancient icicles drooping from
the ceiling and reaching up from the floor. A shallow
pool reflected the snowy whiteness with swirls of rusty
red, creating fairytale castles in the water. It was like a
postcard in its stillness. Then a drip fell into the pool.
Ripples spread gently, mixing the colours like a water-
colour painting. The castle twisted and twirled in front
of Aiden's eyes.

He couldn't be dreaming! It was real, the cave
Dugald had been looking for. Dugald had never seen it,
but he knew it was there. He'd given his life for it.

'This is *your* cave, Dugald,' said Aiden. 'I won't tell
anyone you never made it.'

Now Aiden had more work to do. There might be
another tunnel leading from Dugald's cave. It was Aiden's
only chance of escape. With a new spurt of energy, he
crashed the chisel into the rock. Stroke after stroke he
hacked into the wall. Slowly the limestone fell away till
he could push his head and shoulders through the hole.
He pulled himself through the opening and stood up.

Being there took his breath away. No one had been
here before. Only him. 'You were the sort of guy to

do it, Dugald, not me.'

Mum and Steve and Sabina would never believe it. Suddenly he knew the most important thing was to get back to his family. He had to survive.

He glanced around the cave. It didn't appear to be very big, or to lead anywhere. The ceiling was high above his head, though clusters of stalactites hung low about him like giant chandeliers. He pressed his hand against the outer rock and clambered between the encrusted columns, searching for a tunnel leading from the cave.

With each step, he gasped at the wonder of it. No sculptor could mould a scene like this. It was a magical place. He wanted to hold every moment, yet he couldn't stay.

The rock walls enclosed the cave in a small world of its own. No tunnels led off from anywhere. The ceiling, too, was a solid clot of stalagtites, too dense to open into any sinkhole.

He'd have to go back. Back to where? He didn't want to think, but there was no rescue from here.

He unscrewed the base from his torch and used it as a cup to scoop fresh water from the pool. It tasted clear and sweet. He gulped down another cupful, then filled it again. Now, at least he had water to keep himself alive.

believing

WAITING TO DIE. Was this what it was like?

Don't be stupid! That's what Bryony would say; Sabina too. He had a long way to go yet. Six days, perhaps? You could survive on water for six days, and as long as his strength held, he could crawl back to refill his cup.

Six days. It gave him plenty of time to think. He was here, in the second cavern, staring up the sinkhole at a small notch of sky. He was here, with Dugald close by, so now, at last, the Fisks would have to believe Dugald had gone. They'd be free, and so would he. And Bryony, especially Bryony. The family could finally leave the forest, and maybe one day he'd see her again in the city.

He supposed he'd get used to the smell. He might never get out of here. Dugald didn't.

Sabina once told him that when you're drowning your whole life flashes before your eyes. This was a longer, slower way to die. Flashes of home kept intruding on his thoughts. Mum would be there with Sabina now, but she wouldn't be asleep. She'd be waiting for the telephone to ring. Or she might prowl around the house, looking for things that needed doing; like picking all those white flecks off his tracksuit pants because someone left a tissue in their pocket. Whenever Mum was late for an appointment, it was because there was a tissue in the wash. He could see her as she was last week, picking the specks, bit by bit, off all the clothes. 'I'll go out and give them a good shake,' Steve had said, and come back later looking as if he'd been in a snowstorm.

You could die in snowstorms, too, but Sabina said she'd rather drown. Down here, it was hard to believe that Sabina had upset him so much. She was part of his life and he wanted it to stay that way. He'd felt she was pulling away from him, when maybe she was just growing up. He supposed he was growing too, though he hadn't noticed it. You can't stop people from growing, unless . . .

Unless they were stranded in a cave with no way of escape. He shivered. The cold space inside him swelled and only his family could fill it. If he ever got out of here, he wouldn't take any notice of Titch. He should never have listened to him. He'd made Aiden look at things all the wrong way.

Steve often said to him, joking about other things, 'You believe what you want to believe,' and it was true.

And sometimes you believed what you *didn't* want to believe. He hadn't been strong enough not to believe what Titch told him.

At least, here, he had time to unthink a few things. And to understand. Underground.

Words were playing games inside his head. No wonder, he thought. He didn't have much else to play with down here.

Perhaps he'd fallen asleep, for when he glanced up the shaft, he saw a patch of blue and knew another day had come. It must be Monday. They'd be looking for him. But the ranger was, already! Aiden was becoming confused. The past twenty-four hours were a strange blur, where other people were larger in his memory than himself.

The Fisks would be looking, and Bryony. Steve and Dutchy and Titch would be searching with the ranger.

By now, they were probably dragging the river. But they all knew he was a strong swimmer. Even Titch said Aiden could beat him at freestyle.

In the gloom, he tested his torch batteries again. He had to save them, for while he had light, he had hope. He turned his head, forcing himself to look up the tunnel again to the remains of someone who was never his friend.

'You're a powerful person, Dugald. I felt the pull. From the start, all the time, this is where I was heading. You were pretty brave, coming down here on your own. Steve says that's what makes heroes, doing what other people are afraid to do.

'You were nearly there, Dugald, so close. If only you'd told someone where you were going that night. Or if your parents had let people go through the things in your room. I had your map, you see. That's how I knew about this place. You brought me here, Dugald. Did you want me to find you? You . . . and your cave?'

He stared into the tunnel where Dugald lay and shook his head as he found himself speaking out loud. A tremor ran through his chest. I can't believe I'm here in this musty cave with . . . with . . . with Dugald.

good and bad thoughts

PEOPLE WALKED THROUGH his mind while he tried to stay awake. They came and talked to him and went away before he had a chance to get close to them.

Sabina kept hobbling past, telling him not to worry, she'd only be in plaster for six months. Months? She must mean weeks, he thought. Or was she playing games with him again?

Bryony flitted around the cave, asking questions.

'Why don't you show me things?'

'I can't come now,' he answered.

She pulled a face at him.

'Don't be like Sabina,' he said.

'Who's Sabina?'

He felt too weary to tell the whole long story. 'Someone I know.'

'You knew her while you were away!'

'Sort of . . .'

'I know, *she* was the one who cut your hair!'

'What!'

'*Someone* must have cut your hair.'

Bryony had this strange way of seeing things. 'Don't go now,' he said, but she disappeared before he told her he wasn't Dugald. There was too much to tell. He was exhausted at the thought of it.

Sabina sent a message! Someone had told him so. Why? What would she have to say to him? 'Thanks a lot, Adey.' Or, 'I hope you break a leg, too.'

He'd never told her he was sorry. Nobody gave him the chance, really. Steve had whisked him off on this trip, as if he'd be better out of the way. Maybe he should laugh it off with a friendly message, like 'Can I autograph your plaster?' He knew Sabina; she'd come back with something like, 'Get lost, Adey!'

He was making things up in his head. Still, if he ever got out of this, he'd say he was sorry.

He pulled off his wet boots and stretched his toes. The socks were damp too. He should have brought a spare pair with him. He remembered he'd left an old pair back at the cottage. Until they were darned, they'd been his favourite socks. All at once, he knew why Mum had mended them. She'd sat all evening, missing the best parts of the TV, not to save buying new ones but because they were his favourites.

They'd even joked about her sewing. 'What's this?' Steve had said. 'Darning socks!'

She'd smiled into her hands because she knew they knew she wasn't the type to mend socks.

'Aiden could do it himself,' said Steve.

Aiden walked off in a huff, partly because Steve had made a dig at him, but mostly because he'd been hoping for new socks.

You feel pretty bad when you've been thinking wrong things about someone, especially when that person's your Mum. When he got home, he'd never let on that her darning had given him blisters.

looking and listening

IF HE SHOUTED, would searchers hear his voice? Aiden didn't know whether sound travelled up or down. Would he hear people who might call from above? It was hard to believe any noise could get through the huge weight of earth that lay over his head.

Dugald must have shouted. He would have cried out and cried out till his voice mingled with the cry of the karris, and no one heard. No one came. What happened to the relics of people's cries? Did they just fade on the wind till they were nothing?

Aiden sat with his head still and opened his ears to the sounds about him. The cave was silent, so silent, yet from somewhere came the cry of the forest. Now it was faraway, trapped in the graveyard where cries go; then it was near, so close that it could have come from inside his head.

This cave might have been here, undiscovered, for thousands of years. The thought made him shiver. Only Dugald had known about it, and now him. Other searchers may never find it. The cave lay far off the walking tracks, hidden in the depths of the forest. Aiden had pushed through the densest bush to get here, and only traced it with the help of Dugald's map.

Now he could do nothing but wait. He stretched his legs and walked in a circle one way and back again, as many times as he could endure without flopping to the ground. He must not give in to sleep again.

How long was it, he wondered, before Dugald gave in to sleep? This shabby cavern was a miserable place to die. There was nothing beautiful here, no jewelled candles, no pearly shawls or reflective pools. Dugald had died disappointed. 'I'll never tell them, Dugald,' he said.

Watching the sky became Aiden's chief occupation. The picture from the tiny opening changed with each hour, now blue, now paling to white and then scrubby grey. At times he was afraid he'd drifted into sleep, for the patterns changed like a kaleidoscope.

Looking and listening were all that could save him. He took another sip from his makeshift cup and stared at the passing of the day. A shadowy film stole across his window. As the afternoon dimmed towards evening, Aiden steeled himself to face another night.

Night came soon, for as he stared up, a deep shade blotted out the sky. It was as if a lid had been placed on the shaft. Then, just as quickly, the shadow lifted and another passed over him. Something was moving out there. Kangaroos, perhaps, or foxes.

A flicker of light crossed the sinkhole and was gone. Aiden leapt to his feet. Animals didn't carry lights! He grabbed the torch and held it high, shining the beam straight up the shaft. The night he dreaded might be his saviour. 'Here! Look here! Hey! Hey! Here!' he shouted till his throat was hoarse. He switched the torch off, then on again. Surely, its beam could reach the top and send just the faintest signal into the night. 'Please look! Please, please.' Off and on. Off-on. 'Come on, please!' Someone must be up there. Had they gone away?

The opening darkened, and he thought he heard a voice. His mind was deceiving him. Then a face peered down from the top. It was definitely a face. 'Is someone down there? Who's there?' said a man's voice. 'Aiden? Aiden?'

'Can't you see me, I'm here!' he called back. 'We're here.'

free

A PAIR OF legs dangled from the top of the shaft. Heavy boots dug into the wall as a man lowered himself on a rope. His feet touched the floor of the cave, and he turned to face Aiden. 'You're safe.'

Aiden knew this was the ranger. 'I'm Aiden,' he said.

The ranger smiled, as if he didn't need to be told. 'We'll have you out of here in no time.' He slipped from his harness and moved to help Aiden into the straps.

Aiden stepped back and shone his torch into the corner of the cave. 'There is . . . there's someone else . . .'

The ranger placed both Aiden's hands on the rope and covered them with his own. 'I thought it might have been something like this.' His voice was soft. 'But right now, we're getting *you* out of here.'

'I never thought anyone would find us.'

'You've got to be lucky, yeah,' said the ranger. 'The girl led us here.'

Bryony! Bryony knew what Dugald was up to, thought Aiden.

'She found a map, back on the track. She was out looking for you. We've been looking since first thing Sunday, and at last we caught your signals.'

'I saved my batteries for that.'

The ranger tugged on the rope and shouted up the shaft. 'Okay, coming up!'

Nearing the top, Aiden heard voices. But when his head broke through the opening, the talk changed to clapping and cheers. He scrambled to his feet, and saw Steve standing there, white-faced in the night. In a moment, he felt Steve's arms around him. 'Thank goodness you're safe.'

'Sorry, Steve,' he whispered, and couldn't think what else to say.

'Ssh! Ssh, no worries. We've got you back, that's all that matters.'

Aiden looked around and saw that he was surrounded by strange faces. All these people had come, searching for him. He felt a pang of guilt, for he hadn't wanted to cause all this trouble. Then Dutchy was at his side, his pudding face drained with worry. 'You really are all right?'

Aiden nodded. He'd think about his shoulder later.

'But why . . . why did you do it?'

It was a story too long to tell. 'I was looking for something,' he said.

Titch was there, too. He gaped into the sink hole, where Aiden had come from. 'I'd *never* go down there, no way! Wouldn't have the guts. How'd you do it?'

Aiden almost wanted to say, 'It was nothing,' but decided to be honest. 'Don't think I'll be doing it again.'

'Nah!' Titch grinned. 'And me, never.'

Steve's arm was still around his shoulder, as if to reassure Aiden that he didn't have to talk. But Aiden needed to ask, 'I heard . . . was there . . . have you heard from Mum and Sabina?'

'Of course,' said Steve. He felt in his pocket. 'There's a message from Sabina. I wrote it down.'

'What's it say?' Aiden couldn't see in the dark. He unfolded the paper and shone his torch on the words.

Hey, Adey! I know you're out there. A guy like you doesn't get lost. Get found, Adey, and come home, love Sabina.

'Thanks, Steve.' He pushed the message into his coat pocket. 'Gee, my clothes are all wet. I stink a bit, too.'

Steve's face was still pale, but he smiled. 'More than a bit.'

Someone lowered the rope again for the ranger. Aiden searched the faces gathered about him, and saw Bryony standing away from the others, with her parents. She clutched her mother's arm, holding her back.

'Steve,' said Aiden, 'I want you to come . . . meet the people who looked after me.' When he saw Bryony's eyes, he knew he didn't have to tell her.

'Hello, Aiden,' she said.

'Hi, Bryony, this is Steve.'

She smiled as if she already knew him, for they had passed along the trail.

'The ranger told me,' said Aiden. 'You showed them the way.'

'I found the map back near the Crooked Tree.' She edged closer to him and whispered. 'I knew you'd go out last night. You had that look in your eye.'

'I had to,' he replied. Perhaps, now was the time to tell her. 'Bryony, there's something . . .'

'I think I know.'

'Something you must see.'

'Please, not now.'

Of course, she was thinking of Dugald. 'No, no, I don't mean now. It's Dugald's Cave, he found it!'

Her mother and father hung back, as if somehow they didn't belong. As Steve held out his hand to them, the ranger pushed through the crowd. 'You'll have to excuse me. Could I talk to Mr and Mrs Fisk for a minute?'

He drew them aside and spoke in low tones that no one else could hear. When they came back to the group, clasping Bryony's hands, their faces told that all their hopes and all their doubts had been washed away. They stood for a moment without speaking, then Mrs Fisk stepped towards Aiden and took his hand.

'Goodbye, Aiden,' she said.

He bowed his head, knowing that in saying goodbye to him, they were letting go of Dugald, too.

Bryony gazed up at Aiden with her calm blue-green eyes. 'So it's ended,' she breathed. But as she walked away with her parents' arms circling her shoulders, he could see that it was also a beginning.

For all of them.

about the author

ERROL BROOME CAN'T remember when she began making up stories. She won her first award for writing at the age of nine. As a child in Perth, she was a regular contributor to *The Western Mail* children's pages. After a career in journalism, she turned to fiction and has published many books for children. Errol's writing is noted for its vivid portrayal of the daily dramas of children's lives.

Errol Broome's first novel for Allen & Unwin, *Dear Mr Sprouts*, won the 1992 Western Australian Premier's Book Award for children's fiction and was shortlisted for the 1992 Mulitcultural Children's Literature Award. Her books *Tangles, Rockhopper* and *Nightwatch* have also been short-listed for the Western Australian Premier's Book awards.

When she is not writing, Errol spends her time working in the garden. She lives in Melbourne with her husband. They have three grown-up sons and an expanding family.